P9-CTO-789

A NOTE TO PARENTS

When your children are ready to "step into reading," giving them the right books is as crucial as giving them the right food to eat. **Step into Reading Books** present exciting stories and information reinforced with lively, colorful illustrations that make learning to read fun, satisfying, and worthwhile. They are priced so that acquiring an entire library of them is affordable. And they are beginning readers with a difference—they're written on five levels.

Early Step into Reading Books are designed for brand-new readers, with large type and only one or two lines of very simple text per page. **Step 1 Books** feature the same easy-to-read type as the Early Step into Reading Books, but with more words per page. **Step 2 Books** are both longer and slightly more difficult, while **Step 3 Books** introduce readers to paragraphs and fully developed plot lines. **Step 4 Books** offer exciting nonfiction for the increasingly independent reader.

The grade levels assigned to the five steps—preschool through kindergarten for the Early Books, preschool through grade 1 for Step 1, grades 1 through 3 for Step 2, grades 2 through 3 for Step 3, and grades 2 through 4 for Step 4—are intended only as guides. Some children move through all five steps very rapidly; others climb the steps over a period of several years. Either way, these books will help your child "step into reading" in style!

To Ron and Marilyn
—F.M.

Text copyright © 2000 by Frances Minters.
Illustrations copyright © 2000 by Diane Greenseid.
All rights reserved under International and Pan-American Copyright Conventions.
Published in the United States by Random House, Inc., New York, and simultaneously
in Canada by Random House of Canada Limited, Toronto.

www.randomhouse.com/kids

Library of Congress Cataloging-in-Publication Data
Minters, Frances.
Chicken for a day / by Frances Minters ; illustrated by Diane Greenseid.
p. cm. — (A step 2 book)
SUMMARY: A girl wakes up to find she has turned into a chicken.
ISBN 0-679-89133-1 (pbk.) — ISBN 0-679-99133-6 (lib. bdg.)
[1. Chickens—Fiction.] I. Greenseid, Diane, ill. II. Title. III. Series: Step into Reading.
Step 2 book. PZ7.M67335Ch 2000 [E]—dc21 98-10188

Printed in the United States of America August 2000 10 9 8 7 6 5 4 3 2 1

STEP INTO READING, RANDOM HOUSE, and the Random House colophon are registered
trademarks and the Step into Reading colophon is a trademark of Random House, Inc.

Step into Reading®

Chicken for a Day

by Frances Minters

illustrated by Diane Greenseid

A Step 2 Book

Random House 🏠 New York

Daisy at Home

One morning,

Daisy woke up and

found she had turned into

a chicken.

She flopped out of bed.

She hopped to the mirror.

She had black-and-white
feathers.

She had a yellow beak.

She was a chicken, all right.

A big one, too.

Daisy flapped her chicken wings.

She scratched the rug

with her yellow chicken feet.

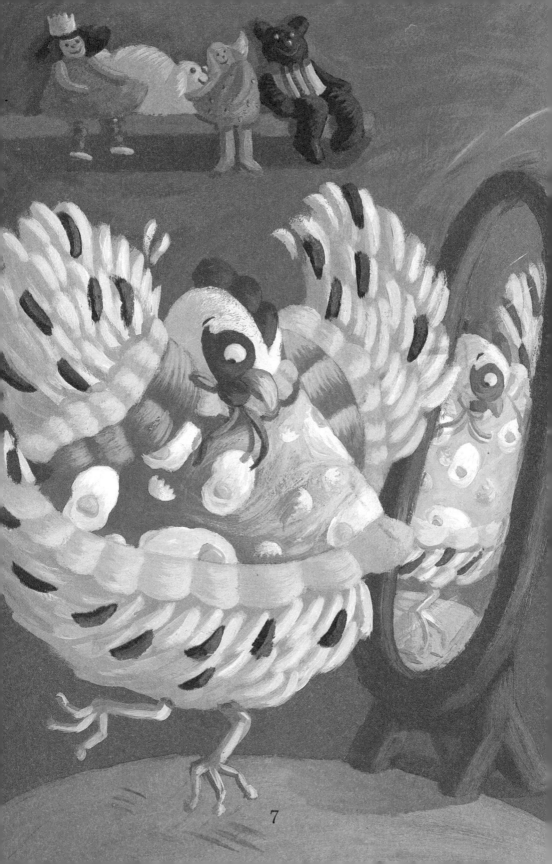

7

Daisy strutted
into the kitchen.
Her parents were
eating breakfast.
"Oh, my," said Mother.
"Daisy has turned
into a chicken."

"Did you brush your teeth?"
asked Father.

"Cluck," said Daisy.

"Chickens don't have teeth,"
said Mother.

"You're right," said Father.

"Daisy, go wash your wings."

Daisy hopped

into the bathroom.

She flew up to the sink.

She turned the tap on

with her beak.

10

The water felt yucky
on her feathers.

"It's not easy being a chicken,"
thought Daisy.

Daisy went back to the kitchen.

She flew onto her chair.

"How about an egg for breakfast?"
asked Mother.

Daisy shook her head.

"Oops! Pardon me,"

said Mother.

"How about cornflakes?"

Daisy nodded.

Father placed a bowl
in front of Daisy.
Daisy stuck her head in it.
"Use your spoon," said Father.
"Chickens don't use spoons,"
said Mother.
"You're right," said Father.
Daisy pecked at her cornflakes.
Yum, yum!
They were good!

Daisy on the Bus

It was time to go to school.

Daisy clucked good-bye.

"Have a nice day,"

her parents said.

The school bus was waiting.

Daisy flapped up the steps.

"Stop!" said the bus driver.

"See that sign?"

The sign said: NO ANIMALS!

Daisy tried to say,

"I'm not a REAL animal."

But what came out was,

"Cluck!"

"I'm sorry,"

the driver said.

"You have to get off."

Daisy hopped off the bus.

What would she do now?

Then she had an idea.

Daisy at the Farm

Daisy decided to go
to a farm.
She wanted to find
other chickens.
"Maybe there is
a chicken school,"
Daisy thought.
"I could learn how to be
a REAL chicken."
She started walking.

After a while, she saw a farm.

She went in.

Some chickens were jumping
in and out of a basket.
Daisy wondered why.

"Cluck!" said a hen.

Daisy understood.

The hen had said,

"They are playing basketball."

"Oh!" said Daisy.

The hen was pretty,

for a chicken.

"I'm Mona," she said.

"I'm Daisy," said Daisy.

"I used to be a girl,

but now I'm a chicken."

"Then you're not a

REAL chicken," said Mona.

"No," said Daisy.

"I'm here to learn."

"Then watch me," said Mona.

Mona scratched the ground.

She pulled something up.

"Here is a juicy worm for you

to eat," said Mona.

"No, thank you,"

Daisy said politely.

"I just had breakfast."

Mona ate the worm in one gulp.

"REAL chickens eat worms,"

said Mona.

Mona took Daisy into the barn.
She pointed at little swings
that hung from the ceiling.
"Those are called perches,"
Mona said.
"We sleep on them."
They did not look comfortable.

Daisy flew up and

wrapped her toes around

a perch.

She swung back and forth.

It was fun.

"Good!" said Mona.

"Almost as good

as a REAL chicken."

"Shh!" said Daisy.

She had heard something.

Then she saw it.

Oh, no! It was a fox.

Foxes EAT chickens!

"Mona, run!" Daisy shouted.

"There's a fox in the barn!"

"Eek!" said Mona.

She ran,

but the fox was faster.

He grabbed her in his mouth.

Daisy had to do something!

Daisy held on to her perch

with one foot.

She swung back

as far as she could go.

Then she swung forward.

With her free foot,

she kicked the fox.

She scratched him
with her long, sharp
chicken toenails.
The fox opened his mouth.
He dropped Mona.
"Ouch!" he said.

The other chickens
had heard the noise.
They came running.

"Don't just stand there
with your beaks open,"
said Daisy.
"Form a circle around the fox."
They did.

"Fox," said Daisy,
"we will let you go
if you promise
never to harm
another chicken.
If you don't, we will
scratch you."

The fox looked at the
angry chickens.
"I promise," he said.
"Then go!" said Daisy.

He went.

"Thank you, Daisy,"

said Mona.

"You saved my life."

"That's all right,"

said Daisy.

"Real GIRLS

help their friends."

Daisy Returns

Daisy was ready to go home.

"Will you come back tomorrow?"

asked the REAL chickens.

"No," said Daisy.

"I want to be a girl again."

The chickens waved good-bye.

When she got near home,

Daisy felt her legs grow longer.

She felt herself get taller.

She rushed into her house.

She looked in the mirror.

Yes, it was true.

She had skin,

not feathers.

She had arms,

not wings.

She was a girl again!

Her parents came in.

"Oh, my," said Mother.

"Daisy is a girl again."

"You're right," said Father.

"Cluck!" said Daisy.

Mother looked at Father.

Father looked at Mother.

"Just joking," Daisy said.

"That's good, dear,"
said Mother and Father.

Daisy gave them a big hug.